written by
REYAANSH JOSHI

An Alien's Biography:

LIFE
ON
EARTH

This edition first published in paperback by
Michael Terence Publishing in 2023
www.mtp.agency

Copyright © 2023 Reyaansh Joshi

Reyaansh Joshi has asserted the right to be identified as
the author of this work in accordance with the
Copyright, Designs and Patents Act 1988

ISBN 9781800946736

No part of this publication may be reproduced, stored
in a retrieval system, or transmitted, in any form or
by any means, electronic, mechanical, photocopying,
recording or otherwise, without the prior
permission of the publisher

Cover design
Copyright © 2023 Michael Terence Publishing

An Alien's Biography: Life on Earth

"Hey, Buckay! Wake up; it's time to meet your older brother," Buckay's mother called out.

"Mother, why? I was right in the middle of a wonderful dream. Can't we go tomorrow?" he replied weakly, still half-asleep.

"Sorry, Buckay, but today we've reviewed all the asteroid forecasts, and there's going to be an asteroid rain tomorrow in the Andromeda Galaxy," she explained.

"Can't we delay it till the day after tomorrow?"

"No, Buckay," his father chimed in.

"Don't worry, you'll have plenty more dreams," his mother reassured him.

"Yes," said his father, "you'll have many more beautiful dreams, but for now, let's prepare for our journey!"

"OK, all right," Buckay replied with a yawn, still shaking off his sleepiness. With a somewhat discontented expression, he finally roused himself. He brushed his teeth and had his breakfast. Afterwards, he headed out to play alien tag with his neighbours.

As the clock struck 10 a.m., it was time for them to depart.

Buckay, an alien, was journeying to the Galadia planet located in the Andromeda Galaxy. His purpose was to reunite with his twin brother, Luckay, who held the distinction of being a mere 2 minutes older. The anticipation had been building within Buckay to visit his brother for quite some time. As he joined his parents on this adventure, his excitement was palpable. This journey also marked the farthest venture from his home city, making the prospect of meeting his brother even more thrilling. The notion of exploration and the chance to visit Luckay's residence had always held a strong allure for him. The images of their abode, glimpsed through their UFO communicator, had only heightened his fascination.

Buckay had always been intrigued by asteroids, considering them to be wonders of the universe. Despite their potentially dangerous nature, he viewed them as nothing more than small pebbles floating through space at high speeds. This perception was likely due to their appearance from a distance, but he knew they were substantial.

Each inhabitant of the alien planet possessed a single UFO, as there was no room available for two in any of the UFOs on their planet. This intentional design included a button that could shrink the UFO to a pendant size.

Soon, they reached the asteroid belt of the Andromeda Galaxy which we know as the Milky Way. A danger alarm, indicating something 700 miles up ahead, flashed on Buckay's communicator. It was a clear signal for immediate action. Luckily for him, his parents were close by, and he knew he could count on their support.

His father reached out to him through the communicator, "Son, listen very carefully. There is danger approaching from the east that seems to be a significant impact. Exercise caution, and with luck, we might navigate through this unexpected asteroid ambush."

"I agree with your father," said his mother. "I know you can do it. Just keep your eyes on the asteroids."

"Yes, yes, I understand, father and mother. I will dodge them; don't worry."

As they continued their journey, Buckay was mesmerized by a dazzling, nebula-like star radiating magnificent shades of blue and gold. However, his fascination was abruptly interrupted when an enormous 17-foot asteroid from the asteroid belt collided violently with his UFO.

Due to the collision, Buckay was carried towards Mars. He searched desperately for his parents but unfortunately, their UFO was also adrift in space. The sight of their damaged craft left him stunned and overwhelmed by a profound sense of loss. Clasping his fingers, he fervently hoped that they were safe and that they would all be reunited soon.

Buckay endured a challenging period as he struggled with helplessness and isolation due to the damaged UFO. Undoubtedly, being separated from his parents and unable to communicate with them constituted an incredibly difficult experience. He felt a profound sense of sadness as he reflected on the fact that they should have heeded his suggestion to wait until after tomorrow's asteroid fall.

"Ahhhhh!" he screamed with all his might, hoping against hope that someone might hear him. Then, a realization struck him; sound didn't travel in the vacuum of space.

He waited for two long days, his desperation growing as he anxiously hoped for a response from his parents. He made several attempts to call them, but to no effect; the situation was deteriorating. It became increasingly clear to him that his UFO's transmitter must have suffered severe damage, leaving him unable to make calls or send messages. He pondered the possibility of being stranded on the planet indefinitely.

Finally, he spotted his parents' UFO gradually moving towards an almost invisible planet. Overcoming the difficulty of reaching it, he maintained a positive outlook due to his father's scientific expertise, which he believed would provide a solution. He was surprised by his bad luck as his mother and father were floating towards the same planet while Buckay was alone on this red planet.

Ultimately, he determined that it was imperative to assume control and commence a journey to scour the planet for something of worth. Regrettably, his expedition produced nothing but debris; no vegetation or any other useful objects were discovered. Then he remembered his father's advice:

When you crash into a planet or a moon or get hit by an asteroid, just search for resources. If the planet/moon you crashed into does not have resources, just find the nearest planet. Also, don't forget the PAMSL to find planets and metal resources. **PAMSL is your planet and metal resources locater.**

As he scoured the Martian terrain for a rover, it suddenly dawned on him that his GPS device boasted the ability to locate electronic items, metals and even planets. He wasted no time in activating the PAMSL and moving at least seven meters away, with the hope of catching a signal. However, his efforts were in vain as he discovered that all the rovers were situated on the opposite side of the planet. With this realization, he felt a wave of discouragement and sadness wash over him, but he knew he had to make his way back to his UFO, which was no easy feat.

As he started to search Mars further, he found an amazing shiny blue stone! A diamond! He decided to keep it with him as a memento. So, he dropped the idea of searching for rovers and decided to search for nearby planets instead, looking for more help.

On checking his GPS, Buckay observed Jupiter, the nearest planet to Mars, though devoid of any land or life. Further on, Saturn came into view, followed by Earth, the planet closest to Mars that sustained life. He finally decided that he must go to Earth. He remembered that he had a reserve tank for these situations.

Being a child, Buckay failed to consider the possibility of using reserve fuel to fly to the rovers and take their fuel. However, as it happened, the fuel available in the rovers wasn't compatible with his UFO, which would have made it a wasteful endeavour. He did recall learning about a big blue planet in school that was the closest to their present location and knew a common language. It dawned on him that his grandfather was trapped there, and he missed him terribly. Buckay resolved to travel to that planet.

After inspecting his reserve fuel, it became apparent that he lacked the required amount to complete his journey. Despite having a substantial quantity, additional fuel was needed to reach his intended destination. He had to resume his search on the planet immediately, despite the harsh, cold conditions. Fortunately, his suit was designed to withstand such environments and allowed him to continue his search without delay.

He was suffering from loneliness and started thinking of his parents' faces. Finally, he decided to use as much fuel as he had and take the risk. He proceeded with his journey, but to his astonishment, he spotted an unidentified object revolving around Earth. It turned out to be a satellite in orbit. The mere thought of encountering asteroids terrified him because he wouldn't be able to manipulate or direct the UFO. Fortunately, no asteroid obstructed his route and he proceeded with his voyage to Earth.

By this time, he had totally forgotten about the diamond. He went on until finally, the UFO started to slow down. It soon became apparent that he was on the correct trajectory towards Earth and would not be landing in a body of water. Furthermore, he had sufficient speed to reach his desired destination.

As he entered the atmosphere, the no-gravity feeling disappeared and after crashing his UFO into a small, abandoned area, he cautiously surveyed his surroundings to ensure he hadn't been spotted. He realised he had landed within the confines of a dense forest and quickly transformed himself into a human being.

He started to look around the UFO to find out which part had been damaged, but it only had a dent where the asteroid had hit it. He quickly pressed the UFO convertor button and transformed it into a small stone, which he immediately hung around his neck as a pendant.

He quickly took his UFO's Planet Location Finder, (PLF) and found out that he had landed in India, in a place called Karnataka, Bengaluru. He thanked his Planet's UFO design and his teacher who taught him how to drive it, as well as his own skills, for not landing in the ocean.

As he looked around, he was quite surprised by the beauty of the city. The grass was long and there were leafy and strong woods, called trees, with a path through them for walking. As for the languages, well while travelling from the Mars to Earth, he had managed to upload all the communication information and found out they had 300 different languages. Mainly he downloaded English, Kannada and Hindi, for now. And he knew the people looked so different here. He studied precisely the various important parts of the Earth and important chemicals and science until finally, he felt ready to communicate with Humans.

After walking cluelessly for some time, he found his way to the city and then tried to communicate with people. He was aware that the beings living on this planet were called humans, people and so on.

"Hello, uh could you erm tell me how to get some fuel?" Buckay asked a man.

"No English," the man replied.

Despite not being fluent in Kannada, the predominant language in Karnataka, he effectively conveyed his message in English to other individuals as he confidently approached them, requesting fuel.

"Buy it with money at a petrol station," advised a man.

"What is a petrol station?"

"Huh? It's a place where you get fuel."

He started looking for a petrol station, and when he found one, he saw the kind of fuel he needed was not available at all. Petrol and diesel were definitely not the types of fuel required. His UFO ran on liquid hydrogen, also used in rockets. It was then he realised he would probably have to spend a lot of time on this planet.

He walked around wondering what to do next then suddenly he thought, "Let me check my UFO for some assets for more help."

Despite all his thinking and thinking, he still did not remember about the diamond. He pressed the button to make the pendant big at an abandoned spot and turned it back into a UFO. But he had nothing to use now without fuel.

Buckay's emotions ran high as he envisioned the possibility of never seeing his parents again. Nevertheless, he found solace in the teachings of his educators about the human race's ability to venture into space as astronauts and explore other planets. He started to ask people how to become an astronaut.

As one woman was passing by, he asked her, "How can I become an astronaut?"

"Uh, if you're in school ask your teacher, kid," she replied.

"But I don't go to a school."

"OK then, uh you have to be an adult and need to learn a lot of science and get a job in any space company like NASA, SpaceX and ISRO which I doubt you might get as many people are turned down."

"Thank you so much for informing me about this but if you don't mind can I ask you another question?" asked Buckay.

"Uh, fine but hurry up I have to go," she said.

"How can I earn money?"

The woman looked puzzled. "Are you for real, kiddo?" she said. "Run to your parents."

"I lost my parents in a storm and to search for them I need to know how to earn money."

This got her attention. "I must take you to the police station and I am sorry for the situation you are in."

"It's OK," Buckay said.

While walking towards the station Buckay kept asking her about how he could earn money. She told him that he must study first. Then he would be eligible for a job in 12 years as child labour is a crime in India. Buckay got it and decided to see what would happen at the station.

When they arrived, they saw a concerned family approaching the police to lodge a complaint. Their young son had ventured out to play a game of football with his friends and had yet to return. The parents were understandably worried and sought the police's assistance in locating their child. His mom was inconsolable and his father was tense. Buckay felt his parents must be feeling exactly the same about him right now, if only they were safe.

He was lost in his thoughts and at that exact moment, the mother looked at him and gave an emotional smile as if she felt it was her son who had come back. The police had gone to find their son and suddenly Buckay felt a knock on his shoulder and realised a person was trying to talk to him.

The person who was in a khaki uniform, asked him, "Hey, Kiddo, what is your name and where are you from?"

"I am Buckay, and I am from Thermono."

The Policeman did not realize it was a foreign name; he thought it was somewhere in another state, city or country. At the same moment Buckay realised he could not say he was from another planet, nor give the names of his parents. Just as he was wondering what to do next, some noise erupted in the room. The mother was super happy, looking at a boy the same age as him and she was in tears, hugging her son. While father asked him where he had been. The kid said he was playing on a tennis court and lost track of time. He was apologizing to his parents and promised it would not happen again.

Buckay felt so happy that the mother was happy again. Suddenly the Chief Police Commissioner called him and said, "Please describe your town and parents?"

"I don't recall anything," he lied because he didn't know the name of any town or city on this planet.

The kid's father was completing some formalities and suddenly he saw what was happening. He started asking the Commissioner who told him that the boy did not remember anything about the town and his parents and needed to be sent to an orphanage home.

"I would like to take care of his studies if you don't mind until you locate his family?" said the father.

The commissioner was incredibly happy, while Buckay just stood there clueless as to what was happening.

"I will enrol him in a nearby orphanage and a school. We will let you know the bills," said the man.

Suddenly the kid and his mother walked up to Buckay and started chitchatting, about age and all. It turned out that the boy was the same age as him and he looked like a smart kid. He introduced himself as Reyaansh.

After talking to Buckay for some time, he walked up to his parents and asked, "Dad, can you enrol him at my school? It will be so cool."

His father looked at the Commissioner and said, "Please let me know if it's possible. I can make arrangements for his schooling."

Buckay decided he would focus on his studies as he remembered his teachers' teachings and the woman's instructions.

With the help of the Commissioner and Reyaansh's father's support, he went into the orphanage in the nearby school area, so that he could commute by bus. And he got into the school, TCIS in Karnataka, Bengaluru. He was learning to live alone, without his parents; he was learning to live on a totally different planet, with different types of food and different timings. Humans took baths with $H2O$ to keep themselves clean from the pollution created by their vehicles. Humans didn't have UFOs, they had cars, aeroplanes and bikes, 2-wheelers, 3-wheelers and 4-wheelers. They had concrete buildings for living in, square-like structures. He was noticing all this and his mind kept comparing it with his planet's infrastructure. He now realised one thing, he couldn't keep doing this. If he wanted to go back, he needed to acquire knowledge to get what he needed and to face the present with smartness.

On the first day of school, it was a simple assembly outside on the school grounds. Buckay was surprised by the huge football ground.

"So, children, are we excited about the first day of school?" the principal asked everybody.

In India, he noticed people said Ma'am' not Miss. He did not reply but everybody else spoke together so it sounded like they were shouting, "YESSS MA'AM!"

"OK, so as we all know because of COVID, we have been attending school by computer, laptops and mobile or tablets. So now, are we happy that we are finally getting to meet our friends again?" she asked.

"YES, MA'AM!" everybody screamed.

"Ok, so since we have been attending school for a long time online anyway, we have prepared a quiz for you all to solve."

"OK, MA'AM!"

After the questions had all been answered, including by one of Buckay's classmates, they went to class. Obviously, on the first day of school, the teachers gave introductions.

"Woah, so this year we've got hmmm, four nice new students. OK, so my name is Shubha and I am your class teacher, as well as your maths and physics teacher," she said. "What we do is that when a new person joins, we assign them to a person to help them throughout the year. So, you can choose; first, let's go with Reyaansh."

"Me? OK uh, I choose umm…"

"Everyone is looking at you with hope, Reyaansh, choose wisely," said Shubha ma'am.

"Hmm, OK, I choose him," Reyaansh said pointing to Gurucharan.

"OK so if you don't mind, will you come to this seat near Gurucharan?" she asked.

"OK, ma'am," Reyaansh said moving to the seat behind Gurucharan.

"Now, next is Buckay," announced Shubha ma'am. "Who will you choose?"

"OK, me uh I think I'll go with him," replied Buckay pointing to a boy named Sean. (Pronounced Shawn).

"All right so his name is Sean and sorry I forgot to introduce you to Gurucharan, Reyaansh, his name is Gurucharan."

"OK, ma'am," said Buckay and Reyaansh together.

Reyaansh had a habit of asking fun facts every other day and they were remarkably interesting. During recess time, Reyaansh also told a few fun facts to all his classmates.

"So, uh people, I have a fun fact. If you think about it, reading a book is looking at a dead tree and hallucinating," he said.

Everyone gave it a long thought.

"Woah, that's true dude," said Shreya and everyone agreed.

"OK, second," Reyaansh said, "this is basically a question but kinda confusing so, why is bacon called bacon and cookies called cookies if you bake cookies and cook bacon? I'm vegetarian by the way."

Everyone started to think, and it was super silent.

"Maybe the person who named it was not thinking properly?" suggested Shreya.

"Or maybe that the person forgot the fact?" added Shoban.

"I don't know," said Reyaansh, "I am asking you."

"All right, I got it," said Anubhav. "It's because maybe in some other language, it means something else."

"Yeah, that makes sense," Sean said.

"Yeah, that makes *some* sense," everyone started to say.

"But I don't think anyone would name 'cookie' in an ancient language or any other like Greek," Buckay said. "They probably did not even know that the word 'cook' or 'bake' means what it means."

"That's actually true!" Sean said.

"That makes PERFECT sense!" Shobhan said.

"Yeah," Reyaansh replied.

"Now this one is the last; I will think of a few more next time," said Reyaansh. "Is the fruit orange called orange because orange is orange or is orange called orange because the fruit orange is orange? Make it short, which orange came first?"

"That's a lot of oranges you mentioned there," said Sean.

"Yes," replied Reyaansh.

"Hey, I have a question-type fact too!" said Sanvi. "So, water, lemon and sugar are free at a restaurant, but lemonade costs money."

"That's a really good one but lemon costs money," Nainika said.

"OK, so suppose a lemon is 10/5 rupees and lemonade is 30 rupees then?" Sanvi asked Nainika.

"It could be higher," Nainika said.

"For God's sake, Nainika, will you ever agree with me or not?!"

"I wonder," Nainika muttered then she replied, "Sorry I will, OK? Chill."

"OK, I just got one more. So, birthday gifts are just rewards for not dying that year!" said Reyaansh.

"Nice one," replied Sean.

"It's actually a present given to a person as that was the day they were born," Buckay said. "Imagine a 4-year-old on his birthday with PERFECT health, do you expect him to die?"

"Anything can happen?" Nainika said.

"Nainika, enough with your gruesomeness," said Sanvi.

"Yes, Buckay, that's true I agree," added Reyaansh.

Soon the school turned out to be a wonderful place with Buckay, Reyaansh and Anubhav becoming best friends and having a lot of fun together, both in the school and while studying. Buckay was living in a sophisticated orphanage nearby, hence he was able to attend the school because of Reyaansh's father.

After a few months, it was time for their exams. Buckay and Reyaansh had studied hard for these exams together and they got above 20 out of 25 in each one, except for French for Reyaansh and Hindi for Buckay. Reyaansh got like fifteen and Buckay got sixteen in the language. It surprised them as they were studying these languages for the first time.

Buckay visited Reyaansh's home daily and his mother cooked and took care of him like her own. His father was always asking if the Commissioner had any update on his parents' well-being. But as we all know, that was not possible. Buckay was aware that it would take at least 8 years for him to escape this planet unless his parents came searching for him. He often had to remind himself, that they were not dead, just lost.

One day Buckay went to Reyaansh's house and had a conversation with Reyaansh's parents. After some conversation with him, they said, "We can adopt you if you like just until you find your parents."

"You can?" asked a surprised Buckay.

"Yes, why not?" replied Reyaansh's parents.

Reyaansh was happy and cool about it as his mother and father had already asked him if he was okay about having a sibling-type friend.

"Yes, that would be great!" he exclaimed.

Buckay said, "I would be more than happy to live with a wonderful and caring family like yours."

Soon his father completed all the paperwork and adopted Buckay officially. After Buckay was adopted, mother and father asked him, when his birthday was. Since he didn't know what a birthday was, he said he didn't remember. So, his parents decided that the day he was adopted would be his birthday.

"OK, what is the date today?" Buckay asked.

"Remember this, it is the 12th of June," his mother told him.

"What is a birthday by the way?"

"It's a special day when you grow taller and your age increases."

"OK."

He went back home happy to know that he had a special day which would be about him.

From then on, he started living with the family. Reyaansh also had a sister. She was very mischievous and used to annoy both of them. She was just like a sister to Buckay. He remembered his own sister who was still studying on planet Thermono. He enjoyed a good life with the family around him. The schooling was excellent, the circle of friends they formed was great and they played sports together, such as football and tennis.

One day Reyaansh's father came home from the office with the wonderful news that the family was moving to Birmingham UK.

Buckay knew the UFO was worthless due to a lack of fuel. He was worried about immigration; what if his UFO in the pendant got under the scanner machines and alerted everyone of some foreign material? Everything would change if that happened. He decided to check the manual to see if there was any setting which he could adjust before flying. He had to find an isolated place so that he could switch the pendant back into the UFO and check the manuals and notes from the classes. Back in the school on Thermono, they were taught about a few scenarios, but he couldn't remember a single one like this.

Still, he had hope. He felt that he would find something in the manual App. He just needed 30 minutes with his UFO. He found a time when all the family decided to visit a friend's home before shifting to the UK. Buckay asked mother if he could stay home as he felt tired. His mother agreed and once they left, he converted the UFO into a size which fitted his room and checked the App in the UFO. After studying it carefully, he realised that if he completely shut his UFO and defused it, the UFO would not be able to come into contact with anything technical. Buckay always kept his UFO on a certain mode which always allowed it to keep contacting his father's UFO. He changed the settings and then converted the UFO back into the pendant.

Much like Reyaansh, he too would miss his Indian companions tremendously. He decided to take the risk with the UFO. On the journey the flight first had to go via Dubai and then on to the UK. When they finally arrived, the trio, Reyaansh, Buckay and Nurvi felt super-duper excited. They were thrilled that they would get to see Tower Bridge, Buckingham Palace and the London Eye. Reyaansh was looking forward to seeing everything and especially over the moon to see Big Ben. OMG, there were so many things on their list. Reyaansh's parents were equally excited. The house they had finalized would be ready in 3 weeks, so in the meantime, they were living in a nice, serviced apartment.

"This is such a wonderful house!" exclaimed Reyaansh when they eventually moved in.

"I must agree!" said Buckay.

Nurvi was with her parents, while Buckay and Reyaansh had a room to themselves. Their parents applied to the council to put them into a school. Buckay and Reyaansh were hoping to get into the same school together. Their parents were even hoping to get all three into the same school. Soon the council gave the good news and bad news. Good news: Buckay and Reyaansh were in the same school. The bad, I think you already guessed it, Nurvi got into a different school. Buckay and Reyaansh felt excited and happy about their luck. Soon, after a few days, it was time to go to school. They enjoyed shopping for their uniforms and prepared themselves with the school worksheets.

The school was wonderful, and the staff were all welcoming, chill and kind; even their classmates were kind. A buddy was assigned to both of them and they were so kind, attentive and informative.

On the first day, they found their first class was computer studies.

"Woah, that is a big computer room!" said Reyaansh.

"Yeah, I agree," said Buckay.

They started by learning basic HTML.

When the class ended, Buckay and Reyaansh made new friends during recess, Maxi, Riley, Samarth, Josh, Zack and Leroy and they all played football. Reyaansh and Buckay were good at it which helped them to make friends faster. Buckay became friends with Leroy Cox who was particularly interested in science and robotics. He invested all his time in reading about science projects and robots and satellites. He owned a drone as well. Buckay started spending a lot of time with Leroy.

One day, Reyaansh who liked to tell everyone facts, got together with Maxi, Samarth, Josh, Riley, Zack and Leroy.

"Hey guys," he said, "do you want to know a few facts which are types of questions?"

"Sure, go on," replied Maxi.

"So, you know when you're inflating a balloon, even when it's half full it's basically completely full," Reyaansh said.

"Wow!" Samarth said, surprised.

"Now this one is really interesting," said Buckay. "I learnt this myself. Does a straw have 1 hole or 2?"

"I don't know," answered Josh.

"Hey Reyaansh and Buckay, I know something as well," piped up Riley. "So, you know when a country plays another country at football it uses the first 3 letters? So when Sweden plays Denmark is says 'SWE-DEN' and the leftover letters are 'DEN-MARK'."

"That is going to be a rare football match," said Buckay.

"Yes," said Riley.

"I bet you can't explain this, Buckay," Reyaansh said.

"We'll see."

"You know James Bond?" Reyaansh asked. Everyone said yes. "He is the most famous spy, right? So that also makes him the worst spy ever as well!"

"I can't explain anything about that but in theory, yes, you're right since now everyone knows his face people will act differently in front of him," Buckay said.

"I have one too," said Josh. "Well, my friend told me this but who cares? Well, you know Peter Parker, Spiderman who is 16 and has a phone and all. So, when he is upside down does his phone have the auto-turn feature on? If so, that would be annoying!"

They shared a laugh and continued to chit-chat throughout the rest of the break time.

During the weekends, the family went to see the London attractions. Tower Bridge was so beautifully designed and looked great. The London Eye was a little crowded that day so they decided to go on it next time. Then they went to see Big Ben, which was visible from the London Eye and the surrounding area. It was a memorable day for the kids and they loved visiting all the tourist attraction places.

Buckay loved watching the soldiers at Buckingham Palace. While walking from Trafalgar Square to Buckingham Palace, they had an amazing moment in life; they put an umbrella up as it was raining, a car was passing at a fast speed and there was a puddle; at the exact moment Buckay opened the umbrella, the car splashed a whole wave of water which was 90% blocked thanks to the umbrella. Was it a reflex action, some sixth sense or some power? Only Buckay would be able to answer that. He was hoping that Reyaansh would think it was a reflex action, but in reality, he had the power to anticipate the danger 10 seconds in advance and safeguard himself.

They started laughing as that was an epic moment and looked like skill. Others who saw it happen could do nothing but stare open-mouthed.

"That was so epic!" Reyaansh said.

"I know, right!" Buckay exclaimed. "Nice sixth sense!" Buckay was just hoping that Reyaansh didn't figure out about his reflex actions, because he was an alien. They can breathe in any kind of environment and see 360 degrees as well without turning their heads.

After a few months and getting settled in the school and different school studies, they made good friends and started doing well in their studies as well. One day Buckay and Reyaansh started to think that what if they started a company? So, they decided to make some inventions.

"Let's create a thing that will be useful for the people who are interested in studying and doing art with a pen," said Reyaansh.

"Sure, but we will need the materials. How will we get those if our parents won't order it for us?" asked Buckay.

"We don't know that for sure until we ask, right?" said Reyaansh.

"OK fine let's do it," agreed Buckay.

They rushed downstairs, excited.

"Uh, mother, we need some supplies if you can order them because we have decided to start a company and make inventions," Reyaansh asked dramatically.

"What supplies?" asked father.

"Supplies like wires, screws, nails, a screwdriver, batteries etc.," Buckay replied.

"OK, we'll think about it and inform you soon," said mother.

The two boys went back to Buckay's room.

"I told you they might listen to us. Like I said you never know until you try."

"Yes dude, I understand but we still don't know, OK?" Buckay said with a sigh.

"Buckay, Reyaansh come downstairs!" called their father.

They came immediately.

"Yes, father?" Reyaansh asked calmly.

"We have made our decision and before we tell you it, where is Nurvi?" asked mother.

"She is in her room watching Peppa Pig on her tab," Reyaansh replied.

"Ok, I will get her," said Mom.

"So, we have decided to buy all the supplies needed as you both have gotten good grades and are behaving very nicely with your sister and doing your chores and respecting other people," said father. "And we already have screws and screwdrivers."

"YES! I TOLD YOU Buckay!" exclaimed Reyaansh. "Thank you, mother and father."

"Yes, thank you!" said Buckay.

Soon after, their order came and Reyaansh and Buckay started work on a pen that gave light so you could write without worrying if it got dark or not, on the basis that it was better than first buying a new pen and then a lamp.

"Maybe you already have a lamp but I mean yes, you can just turn on the lights but what if there is a power outage, or what if you are too tired to turn on the light?" reasoned Reyaansh.

Their first attempt was a failure; instead of giving light the pen started to make a noise like a buzzer.

"Why did the pen make noise?" asked Buckay.

"Probably hungry," Reyaansh grinned.

They started to laugh when the pen made the noise again. On the next attempt, it gave out light but only for a few seconds, but that still counts right?

"Hey, what are these?" Reyaansh asked looking inside the pen where all the wires were.

"Oh my God that's the mistake we've been making," Buckay said. "That's the tiny colour that shows where that coloured wire is supposed to be attached; as you can see, we've put them in all wrong, so we have to fix it."

They fixed their mistake and feeling proud of themselves, showed it to their parents.

"Wow! I can't believe you guys have actually invented something," said Mom.

"Yeah, we can't believe it either!" said Reyaansh.

"OK, so can we continue to make duplicates and sell them?" Buckay asked.

"Sure," replied father.

They started work on making duplicates of the pen and aimed to sell them for five pounds. (500 rupees)

Looking at their invention achieved without any technical knowledge, their father thought, "Let's put them in a robotic class and the software development class for kids, as they both have similar interests. Let's see how far they can continue and learn. Whenever they get bored, I will stop it. Kids at this age enjoy outdoor sports. They are different."

After a few weeks, they made multiple inventions: potions to heal plants, and finally a small toy UFO in which you could put your figurines and drive it with a remote controller.

One day their father called the two of them and announced, "I would like to give the garage to both of you for your inventions. What do you say?"

"OK if I am gonna be honest, this is Aaaaaaaaaamazing, and now, we have the GARAGE!" shouted Reyaansh.

"Yup, I agree," said Buckay. "I can't wait to work in the garage."

"Wooo!" Nurvi whooped.

Soon life was great and amazing and they set off on their new course of inventions. Buckay asked Leroy to join them as he too was interested in science and inventing stuff. He was super smart at science.

One day, Buckay said, "Why don't we spend some of our earnings? We have been saving for months," he added with a hint of sarcasm. "I bet we have a thousand pounds already, right?"

Buckay was thinking of finding a way to fix his UFO. He had been buying some parts with the help of Leroy and checking if the UFO worked. He did all this once everyone else was asleep. But nothing was working out and it sounded as if he was over-reacting a little.

"Look, saving is better than just wasting it on some random stuff," Reyaansh tried to explain.

"It's not RANDOM stuff!" Buckay said in a high voice.

Buckay always had in mind how to repair his UFO but he still didn't have a clue how to go about it. Soon their argument grew stronger, and they did not speak to each other for two days. Their parents divided their money into three portions: one for Buckay, one for Reyaansh and one for Nurvi, together with father and mother.

Buckay spent all his money and Reyaansh saved, as he said. Buckay bought all the stuff for inventions and Reyaansh saved. If they had been a team, this would have worked very well. But now they were avoiding each other, decreasing their happiness together, so their parents stepped in.

"Reyaansh and Buckay both shake hands and end this war," said father.

"Fine," agreed Reyaansh.

They shook hands, but they still did not end it.

After a while, Reyaansh was going to apologize to Buckay but before he could, Buckay apologized first.

"Reyaansh, I'm sorry I did not listen to you. Please let's not fight anymore?"

"Fine, it's alright. I'm sorry too, because I was rude but let's do our stuff in our own way?"

"Sure, but let's become a wonderful team and not fight?"

"Yeah!" agreed Reyaansh.

They started working together again on inventions. However, when they were still fighting, Buckay got bored and made a few inventions himself. They were a new game app and a bunch of tiny figurines which worked like robots.

Reyaansh and Buckay had a movie night as a celebration of earning money at this youthful age. They were sitting on the sofa watching 'Harry Potter and the Chamber of Secrets.'

The next day was special, the annual school play. Buckay was in Drama and Reyaansh was in Dance and Music. He danced hip hop and played the piano, and Buckay's role was the second main character of 'Scrooge' his name was Cratchit. He had many lines, so he was happy that he had a significant role.

The first performance was piano and Reyaansh played the Harry Potter theme music along with his friend, Emma, to great applause. Then, during Buckay's scene, he too got a big round of applause. Nurvi and their parents were cheering and pretty amazed by the performances and Buckay's confident dialogue delivery. After a while, it was finally time for the hip hop kids to dance and Nurvi was super happy that she had already spotted her brother. After all the performances, it was time for the choir students to come and perform three songs.

Buckay was feeling mixed emotions; he was happy that all the family was appreciating him, but also sad as he missed his own family, his brother and sister.

When they got home that evening, they ate homemade pasta and played many games, including Nintendo. And after that, they all slept.

The next morning, Reyaansh had to go to tennis coaching as he was playing in a tournament. As Reyaansh's birthday was close, Buckay helped mother and father in making and decorating the cake, the day before.

That night the family wished each other good night but Reyaansh had a different style.

"Good night!" Buckay said.

"Good night, sleep tight, don't let the vampires bite, there's no need to fight, let's go to the Isle of Wight, it has a wonderful sight and set the candles alight, so you can have a peaceful night!"

The next day Reyaansh woke up to find the family waiting for him to open his eyes. And they shouted, "Happy Birthday!"

"Thank you, people," said Reyaansh.

"So how do you feel now you're a TEEN?!" mother asked.

"I feel… good."

Reyaansh's birthday was celebrated with the family and everyone gave him their gifts. His father gave him a membership for chess.com. His mother gave him a lot of keychains, which was what he wanted. His sister gave him a toy of hers and Buckay gave him a figurine that looked like Reyaansh.

Buckay joined a chess tournament, as he was pretty good at the game. He won the first round and the second, and the third and the fourth and lost in the semi-finals against an admirable player. His achievement was covered in the Birmingham newspaper and appreciated in the school's assembly.

One day Buckay was feeling like he wanted to learn some self-defence so he told Reyaansh about it.

"OK, let's ask mother and father if we can join a karate class?" Reyaansh suggested.

"Oh my God," Buckay exclaimed happily, "That is the perfect idea!"

"I know, right," Reyaansh said.

They asked mother and father and as you would expect, they enrolled both of them in a self-defence class.

When they went for their first Karate class, they met Leroy there and Reyaansh also started to enjoy his company. While talking, he came to know that Reyaansh and Buckay also kept inventing new things and they were quite good at it, so he decided to show his inventions to them.

They were hanging out one evening and after having pizza, they all went to Leroy's room and they saw multiple awesome inventions. One of them was replacing fuel with decomposed liquid. He kept a few items from the home in a decomposing bucket for kind of 15 days and after adding some different items, it created a liquid. But somehow that idea was not working out.

Suddenly, Reyaansh said, "Why not use 20% of fuel in this decomposed liquid? Your invention is about saving fuel, right? So, let's make it with 20% fuel along with the decomp liquid and see what per-mile average it gives."

Leroy was amazed with the idea. Because he was so obsessed with making it zero fuel, he hadn't even thought of this idea. "Sure," he said. "Let me give a thought to this and let's see."

After watching a movie together, Buckay and Reyaansh's mother picked them up. Reyaansh was highly impressed with what he had seen at Leroy's house. Buckay was happy that Reyaansh had enjoyed meeting Leroy.

A few days later, Leroy met Buckay and Reyaansh in the school at lunchtime and said, "I tried using 20% of fuel to see if it could be equivalent to the one litre of fuel and guess what? It worked! The 20% of the fuel and 80% of my decomposed liquid is in fact giving a mileage of 1 litre of fuel. This is how we can save 80% on the cost of fuel.

"This is HUGE, dude!" said Reyaansh and they invited him for a hanging out and they were kind of going through their inventions. Leroy was highly impressed with the different potions and the small UFO that they made.

"Hey! Why don't we try to send our latest creation to NASA, hmm?" asked Buckay.

"That's a great idea, boss," replied Reyaansh.

"OK?" Buckay said confused.

Their latest invention was a small machine that detected any type of special rocks.

"It might help them find some nice rocks when they send a rover to Mars or any other planet!" Reyaansh said.

"I know," Buckay said.

Soon after, Reyaansh and Buckay decided to contact NASA regarding giving their inventions to them for their research. Buckay remembered his teacher's teachings again: "Humans become astronauts and then they can come into space. If you are ever stranded on Earth, become an astronaut but you've got to abandon your UFO, which is a risk because humans can find out our location just by sitting in your UFO and pressing a button. So, please try not to get stranded on Earth."

"Hm this is probably going to be hard but still I will try to get a job at NASA," thought Buckay.

NASA did not accept their inventions as they had nothing to do with those kinds of inventions; they focused mostly on other planets and space and on finding more planets.

"Oof, but let's still work on inventions that will help NASA find out more about space?" suggested Buckay.

"You read my mind," said Reyaansh. "So, what do we plan on making?"

"Hmm, let's think first," replied Buckay.

"Ooh. Oh, I got an idea; why don't we make like a machine that uh umm err- OK I forgot what I was gonna say," Reyaansh said.

"Haha, it happens to me too!" Buckay admitted.

"AHA! Got it!" Reyaansh said at full speed. "We gotta make a machine that is like a rover but has a sensor and scanner at the bottom of it so that if they want to know anything, they can just take the files from the machine, and they will know what that is."

"I er- did not understand one thing you said; say it slowly please."

"Fine," replied Reyaansh. "We must make a machine that will have a sensor and a scanner at the bottom so that if the people at NASA want to know about the weather or the rock, they can simply scan that rock, or any part of the planet and they will know the weather of like 5 months back. They can take the files, by connecting the drive to the rover which will help them know the details of the rock and the weather that has happened lately. We will call our rover the RnBrover."

"Ah, now I understand. All right let's go with this and I understand why you named it RnBrover."

"Reyaansh and Buckay rover!" said Reyaansh.

It was the 24th of December, Christmas Eve. Reyaansh and Buckay had written down a tiny gift they wanted and put it into a sock, a red one of course. They decorated the Christmas tree and hung the lights around the house.

During the day, the whole family started wishing everyone a merry Christmas, ready for the main day tomorrow, and they enjoyed a few jokes with each other. When Reyaansh and Buckay went out into the garden, father thought it would be funny to record them. While he was recording them, they went out to get the clothes in from the garden, and found something quite unbelievable, a real jingle bell!

"WOAH!" Reyaansh shouted.

"Are our gifts already here?" Buckay asked, confused.

"No, I don't think so," replied Reyaansh.

All of this was caught on their father's camera. Who was going to believe them? They would say it was all set up. But they didn't care; they were happy. Soon it was night, and they went to sleep. At about 8 am, a Santa doll which had been bought as a souvenir started to make noises. The family thought it was a glitch and removed the batteries from it. But an hour later, it made the same noise, and they wondered if it was some kind of Christmas miracle!

Today was Christmas, and they got all the gifts they wanted. Reyaansh got a remote-controlled car. Buckay got an astronomy book. mother and father got a few things, like a pair of socks, (Why? Don't ask me) a pair of gloves, 5 jokes, some prank glasses and stuff, and a few candies.

"I love it!" Reyaansh said as he played with his car.

"Me too!" shouted Buckay. "Did you know that on Pluto, there are ice volcanos?"

"No!" replied everyone, surprised.

This was the best and happiest Christmas they had ever had.

It took them 6 months to finally sell the RnBrove to NASA and it was not easy. NASA was happy about the invention, but they asked them to add some more features. They asked Leroy if they could experiment with his fuel on their rover. Leroy was happy about it, and together they started working on the rover. Reyaansh and Buckay made it with both battery and fuel. NASA was impressed with the fuel as well. They liked the rover's speed, the scanning quality and the speed of sending the files to the drive.

They worked and worked, and they evaluated and finally, it was ready.

NASA was extremely happy that they completed what NASA had asked for so fast and they got a good reward. Soon, news spread all over the country and the world about their making an amazing invention that was bought by NASA, the greatest Space Centre. They became popular around the UK, but they were SUPER popular in school as the news was covered in the local newspaper and TV.

Early one morning, Buckay woke up and forgot it was his birthday.

"Wow, that's a good shiny sun right there," he said processing all the information and going through it. Then it hit him. It was his birthday!

He looked around. His room was the same. Maybe they would celebrate it in the hall? He went through the rooms and realised that no one was home.

There was only a handwritten note,

> 'We will be out for the rest of the day see you boi.'

It was written by Reyaansh because only he would say 'boi'. And he had forgotten that it was Buckay's birthday.

He felt sad as his parents had told him that he would have to remember but what was the point if they didn't remember it themselves?

"WAHOO!" Leroy shouted.

"SURPRISE!" Reyaansh shouted. "Boy, you really thought we left!"

"Ahhhh! You got me," Buckay said. "And hey! Leroy is here too!"

He went to the garage and wow, it was decorated with NASA posters, spaceships balloons, and so on, all stuff about space.

"Wow!" Buckay exclaimed.

Even the cake had a rocket and was followed by a banner reading, 'Happy Birthday Buckay!' in space!

"Wow this is the best... uhm what do you call it? YES, a good day, yeah this is the best day of my life," Buckay told everyone.

"It's your birthday," Reyaansh told him and laughed. He gave his gift to Buckay, it was a controlled rocket that could fly. Reyaansh had built it himself. Mother gave him a book containing all the information about the astronauts that had travelled into space. father gave him 100 British pounds so that he could buy anything with it. Nurvi gave him a helium rocket balloon, and Leroy got him a x50 zoom telescope.

After that, they played some music and had a tiny disco party.

Buckay enjoyed this Birthday a lot.

A few years went by. Reyaansh and Buckay had completed their Year 11 and decided on streams for their graduation. Obviously, as they had similar interests they chose science, with a specialisation in space. Their inventions definitely helped them to get into a good college and together, too. On their first day at college, they met up with Leory and made a team.

Their inventions were sold on Amazon and they started a YouTube channel as well to guide youngsters, to respect the ideas coming into their minds and how to make something out of it. They were about to hit 10,000 subscribers on YouTube and they mostly posted how to use their items.

One night, Reyaansh and Buckay were sleeping in their rooms when a person sent a bunch of robots that only had a single line of eyesight. If you came into that line and it saw your face, it would chase you for your whole life until you were dead. The only way to save yourself, if you had come into the line, was by DESTROYING that robot.

It did see Reyaansh's face and chased him. His sister was eleven at that time and it also chased her and his family. Reyaansh soon found out about the robot and informed his family at once, so mother and father told them all to stay together. But the robots chased them as they had already caught the whole family now in their single line of eyesight.

As they were running, they appeared in a huge maze which Reyaansh and Buckay had built for personal entertainment and soon his mother's hand slipped and they got split up. Buckay, mother and father were together and Reyaansh and Nurvi were together.

Reyaansh could hear their voices. "We will meet in the park; try to get there, okay?!" he recognised his father's voice.

"OKAY!" Reyaansh screamed with all his might to make the robots come to him and not to his parents, so his parents could hear, and the robots chased him. And the robots did come after him.

Reyaansh let go of Nurvi's hand for a second and told her to run with him as his hands were sweating and slippery. He thought she was right behind him but she was not, so he ran back at speed only to see Nurvi standing there with a robot heading towards her.

Reyaansh ran as fast as he could and pushed the robot out of the way, then picked up Nurvi and kept running, but the robot caught up with him, took Nurvi and went underground. Reyaansh was about to break and was just gonna simply run at the robots, but he hardened his heart and went to the park where he started digging in the soil and found Nurvi and the robot. He dug a huge hole, quickly pulled Nurvi out and ran.

"Brother, that robot took me down there," wailed Nurvi. "It was so brown and dirty down there," she said crying.

Reyaansh felt the anger. "Yes, I know but it's okay now don't worry," he said, trying to comfort her, but she started screaming and Reyaansh looked back to see at least 5 robots chasing him as fast as tigers. He decided to dodge those robots as they had very tiny eyesight. "Nurvi, go there, okay? And you will be safe." And so Nurvi hurried off.

Suddenly he heard, "Reyaansh, wake up, you need to go to college!"

It had all been just a bad dream. Pffff!

He started telling his mum about his dream and she said, "Why don't you write it?"

He thought then said, "Mom, I only like to share it with you all."

Buckay remembered his conversation with his mum on the fateful day he travelled for Galadia and he got separated. The sadness was so visible on his face that

Mum and Reyaansh started asking him what happened. And as usual, he ran to his room. They both knew that he was missing his family. Reyaansh's father had kept in touch with the Commissioner through emails, asking for updates on Buckay's parents but gave up after so long.

One day, Reyaansh, Leroy and Buckay were chilling and playing football with friends, when Buckay noticed a dummy and went over to pick it up, but the dummy jumped on him and started pinching and squeezing his skin. Buckay picked him out of his shirt and threw him a few metres away. The robot surprised them with his speed; it was amazingly fast but not faster than them. Buckay and his friends took off running and reached a place which had a big tower. They went to the top of the tower and looked for the robot but could not find him. Suddenly, it was right behind them again; it jumped onto Reyaansh and started chewing his clothes, and then Reyaansh plucked him away from him and threw him down the tower!

They rushed down the tower and found the robot lying there lifeless, so they took off again and reached another tower. They looked back to the first tower and saw the robot standing at the top of it, and sent another robot to kill them. That robot was attached to a string and somehow was able to reach them without a problem.

Reyaansh invented one thread from a safety point of view, which was very sharp at the edges; he wanted to use it to cut that string, but Buckay used his powers first and the robot fell lifeless. Reyaansh kept wondering how that happened as he clearly saw Buckay doing something with his fingers but he didn't react. This time, Reyaansh and his friends picked the robot up and took it home to study how it was made and where it might have come from.

Reyaansh kept wondering about Buckay and his whereabouts and his extreme sixth sense when playing football. Many times he noticed him speaking in a foreign language while sleeping. He decided to speak to him about it and was looking for the right opportunity.

Buckay, Leroy and Reyaansh made new friends and started to play tennis in clubs for physical activities. The three of them loved swimming too. Leroy and Reyaansh noticed that Buckay could actually stay underwater for much longer than usual, maybe five minutes or so and they were amazed.

The trio also took up small projects for NASA from time to time, working at home and making constant inventions. Some succeeded, some failed but the amount of money they received helped them to invent more and paid their college fees as well as funding a good time, enjoying the best of college life.

One day their invention went wrong and almost set the whole house on fire. Their spare napkin pile had caught fire but they took their extinguisher and put it out. Meanwhile, the smoke alarm was blaring loudly.

"I CAN'T EVEN READ MY OWN THOUGHTS!" shouted Reyaansh.

"WHAT?!" shouted Buckay.

"I SAID I CAN'T EVEN HEAR MY OWN THOUGHTS!"

"EVEN I CAN'T HEAR YOU!" screamed Buckay back.

"I meant to say I can't even hear my own thoughts not that I can't hear," Reyaansh explained. "I can very specifically hear you so I thought you could hear me and so I said, I can't even hear my own thoughts. And I am sure you can't even hear what I explained."

They ran out of the room and started to close the alarm and soon the noise stopped.

"I said I couldn't hear you when we were in there," Reyaansh said.

"Oh, I thought you said, I cannot hear you," said Buckay.

Later, at dinner, they had a big conversation.

"What was all that noise about?" asked mother.

"Well, I thought you figured it out, it was fire," answered Reyaansh.

"A fire!?" she asked.

"Yes, but we extinguished it but for some reason, the smoke alarm kept on blaring," said Buckay.

"OK, but it better not happen again or you two are in big trouble, OK?"

"OK," Reyaansh and Buckay said in unison but only Reyaansh saluted.

After a while they went back to making that invention; it was a particularly important one, so they worked on it day and night.

"Hey, wait, add this there and I'll take this one and put it here," Reyaansh said as they were placing their final metal piece to cover the can.

"OK, here," Buckay said.

It was a backup oxygen can for space. It was a success and NASA loved it. After it was done, they enjoyed their life as it was a Saturday.

One day news popped up that there was a UFO sighting in Argentina. So Buckay quickly went to his UFO and found out that the UFO coordinates matched with his planet's. He tried to send a signal but didn't receive any response. He knew he had to be patient. Unfortunately, the sighting was in Argentina, and he was in the UK where he could do nothing but simply watch the UFO but he kept a close eye on the news.

"What should we invent next? I'm out of ideas," he said.

"Hmm. What about a robot that will protect us from other killer robots that keep attacking us?" Reyaansh suggested. Then they both remembered the robot they had brought home for research which they had totally forgotten about until then.

Buckay was enthusiastic about the idea and started his research on the metal body and wiring and the metals that were used in that robot.

"Let's observe this bad boy and invent something good out of it. This was a remarkable robot which attacked us," said Buckay.

"I was about to say the same," replied Reyaansh.

Well, their first contrivance was a big failure; in fact, it tried to attack them. Their second contrivance worked out for a while; it was saying 'hello', 'hi' and all but after a few minutes it too started attacking.

The thirty-third contrivance was the one. It was saying 'hi', 'hello' and whenever you said 'help!' it came towards the noise at once and started looking around to detect any people who had been hurt. It could also scan the weapon to find out who made the attack.

It is true that the third one is usually the charm, but clearly, this was not the third, but the third after 30. They laughed a lot about this.

Buckay and Reyaansh were ready to take a trip to meet Reyaansh's grandmother in India. He loved it there as he played badminton with his friends and his uncle owned a club which he liked to visit.

When they got there, Buckay introduced himself and they had a small chat. Over there the lifestyle was different from Reyaansh and Buckay's. It was quite old-fashioned. But that's what he loved about it. They managed; Reyaansh loved it because he could feed the cows and play with puppies and kittens. Eventually, he would go online and post messages to NASA's invention ideas area.

One day he was playing with a kitten and saw that a part of it was looking weird because of a serious infection, which he found out about when he had finally taught the kitten to give a high five. He was extremely saddened and sent the kitten to the vet at once and waited for the results. The vet said that she needed to undergo surgery. The final bill was two thousand. Reyaansh remembered that he had forgotten to change his currency and went to do that immediately, getting 2000 rupees and paying for the kitten's operation. A day later after the surgery, the vet informed them because of the infection that unfortunately, the kitten had died. Reyaansh and Buckay were extremely saddened by this news and decided to bury the kitten. Her name was Clary, and they were both going to miss her a lot.

Just as they were going home, Reyaansh suddenly heard a 'meow.' It turned out to be an abandoned street kitten and Buckay and Reyaansh immediately got out of the car to help it. They took care of the kitten for a while and then took it to the adoption centre and left it there. Then set off for home.

It was time for food and Reyaansh ate Dal and Rice, his favourite food at his grandmother's house. He also got multiple gifts from them for his birthdays, which they always enjoyed.

Buckay soon started exploring around the building; it was an interesting house indeed. They had the most fun searching for stuff in the house and playing with the things they found. Pretty soon they took their Grandmothers's dog, Mowgli, down to play and Nurvi took her kitten. Reyaansh and Buckay were still sad about the kitten that had died recently and were not able to forget about her.

After a few weeks, they finally had to leave to go back to the UK, but first, they visited Clary's grave and put some flowers on it before going back home.

A week after reaching the UK, it was a fresh morning and nearly time for lunch.

"I'm a bit hungry, what should we eat?" said Buckay.

They got into the car and started for the closest McDonalds. On the way they played 2 or 3 of their favourite songs. Reyaansh loved the song 'Despacito' and Buckay played 'Dance Monkey'. Nurvi said she wanted to hear 'Let It Go' from Frozen. Just as they arrived, a man suddenly came out of nowhere, dashed into Buckay and gave him a note.

"Take care of this note and don't let it get destroyed. Whenever you reach a safe place, read it," he said and then hurried away.

"That was disturbing," said Buckay.

"Yes indeed," replied Reyaansh and they both started laughing.

"Ok, we'd better hurry; I think it will close soon."

"Sure, let's go," said Reyaansh.

"Hi Sir, what would you like to sequence today?" asked the waiter.

"Uhm, I would like to order a large fries, thank you," Reyaansh said.

"I would like to order a Mc Veggie burger," added Buckay.

"Okay, anything else you two desire?" asked the waiter.

"No that's it, thanks," replied Reyaansh. "Hey Buckay, give me that note that guy gave you."

"Sure, here," said Buckay said gave it to him.

'THERE WILL BE A FIRE IN MCDONALDS AND YOU WILL BE THE ONE TO EXTINGUISH IT.'

"Yeah, this guy needs to improve his handwriting."

They waited for a while watching their phones. Finally, their order came and they started eating. Then suddenly they heard people screaming. Buckay decided to investigate. He went around but only saw people screaming for no reason. Reyaansh joined him, eating three fries while investigating.

Soon, they discovered why everyone was screaming. There was a fire in the storeroom. They rushed there and found a member of staff using the fire extinguisher, but he had burnt his hand and couldn't hold onto it. Other staff members were busy emptying the café and one person was calling the Fire Brigade. Buckay seized the extinguisher and put out the fire.

"People these days don't think," Reyaansh said.

"Yeah," agreed Buckay.

Then he remembered the note and thought there was something written on the back too, but he hadn't checked it yet. When they read what was on the back, it said,

"You wanna know how I knew? HAHAHA, well just come to Southampton beach. I will be waiting there for you every day until you come."

"Well, that was interesting. We'll go check it out someday," Reyaansh said.

"OK," agreed Buckay.

During the journey back home, Reyaansh probed Buckay about his longing for his family and urged him to share any memories at any time. Buckay picked up on Reyaansh's knowledge of him being an alien and decided to reveal his secret to him. He was convinced that the recent surge in UFO sightings may be the key to reuniting him with his parents or brother. And he valued the relationship so much that he didn't want to hurt this beautiful family of his. He decided he would share it and was determined to talk to Reyaansh first and then assess his reaction before divulging the news to his parents and Nurvi. He also contemplated informing Leroy, but only after notifying his own family.

Engrossed in his thoughts, Nurvi interrupted and inquired, "What is occupying your mind?"

She also pointed out to Reyaansh that he should not ask such things about his family as it might hurt Buckay. Reyaansh agreed.

One day they were thinking of what to invent when Leroy messaged them about his idea of using oxygen like gas. Buckay and Reyaansh motivated him to dig more into the possibilities. They thought of making a torch, which would work like a walkie-talkie, by flipping the switch.

"That would basically be a phone without the apps and all," explained Leroy.

"Good point," Buckay agreed.

This was a wonderful trio as Buckay and Leroy worked while Reyaansh suggested the ideas and brought them the tools.

Soon it was night and Buckay and Reyaansh had a wonderful dream and enjoyed the night. Then the next day, something weird happened. Buckay was taking his normal stroll around the park, the only thing was, NOBODY was there. There was only a lot of wind, and his hair was blowing.

"What is this?" he thought. "No clouds or anything and yet so much wind?"

He looked around for clues to the fierce wind and found the reason why so much wind was coming.

"This is NOT good," he thought as he saw a big portal. It was a black octagon with a blue outline of flame.

Buckay thought that this was shocking news for the Earth as he believed aliens were about to invade, and he had to inform everybody. However, something made him go into the portal. As soon as he entered, he immediately recognized the power frequency and the power rate with the speed levels of the portal. This was something aliens like him had NEVER seen before.

The first thing that happened was he entered a robotic class. He could not believe what he saw. He looked around again and rubbed his eyes; he was in a classroom! When he looked back, to his surprise he found the portal had GONE! It seemed he had become a small kid again, in year or grade 5. The other kids with him looked like straight-up second graders, but he didn't care.

"This is INSANE!" he thought. "I entered an INSANE, powered portal and I think if I try to tell anyone that I'm not from here, they will call ME INSANE. I think I am going insane. THIS IS ABSOLUTELY INSANE!"

He finally decided to stay and not tell anyone anything. He was obviously the smartest in the class as he was an adult who had just entered this portal to investigate but turned into a KID in a classroom!

"Hmm, this does not look like an alien invasion, so I can chill out," he thought. "Oh yes, I have checked the power frequency and the mathematical coordinates and maybe I could build a portal GPS or maybe a portal maker or maybe both of them combined."

He started working on it secretly and finally, he had made a tiny gun with a GPS on top which could track a portal.

After the school ended, to his surprise three kids tried opening the vent which led to a portal! A few kids in the class that Buckay had not noticed, tried to open the vent and the teacher caught them at it and said, "It will take you the rest of the semester to open that and when you do, we'll just put it back in."

Suddenly, the happiness and excitement on their faces turned into frowns but when they looked at Buckay, they smiled again and came up to him.

"Hi, my name is Mark, and these are my friends, Becky and David; can you help us?"

Buckay looked at him and suddenly he thought that the teacher stopped them for a reason, but with their innocent faces, he could not help it and opened it for them. They thanked him and at once went inside, but that's when the teacher stormed in and was in shock that they had already opened it and made them all come out at once. It did not take David and Mark a moment to snitch on Buckay that he had opened the vent.

"Kid, I am disappointed in you. What is your name?" asked the teacher.

"Sorry, Ma'am, I did not know that opening and entering the vent was forbidden; I shall not repeat my mistake. My name is Buckay."

"I accept your apology, Buckay, but do not repeat that mistake," said the teacher.

Soon the class ended and Buckay was looking around to see what to do next. Becky came up to him and apologised for her friend's mistake. As Buckay was an adult, he was not like a kid who got angry when somebody snitched so he accepted the apology and the two became good friends.

After school ended, Buckay and Becky decided to go through the vent even though the teacher had stopped them. But this time Mark and David were not going to go with them. They waited for Mark and David to leave and then opened the vent as fast as possible and entered and closed it.

"Quite hot in here," said Becky, sweating slightly.

"I must agree," said Buckay who was sweating even more.

Soon to their surprise a lot of wind gushed into their faces.

"Ahhhhhhh, that's good," Becky said.

Buckay at once understood the meaning of this. "Becky, there is something I must tell you. I am not from here; I entered a portal from which I arrived on this land."

"Ha-ha, good joke Buckay. I am surprised," she laughed.

"No, I am serious, and this is definitely another portal, it's the same wind."

"OK and?"

Buckay sighed, "I am serious. I wouldn't believe me either, but you've got to believe me."

Becky did not say anything, and they just continued. Finally, they spotted the portal and entered it.

"What did I say?" asked Buckay.

Becky sighed and nodded.

Everything was in pixels; they did not look like humans, and all the bodies looked weird.

"What is the meaning of this?" she asked.

"I have no idea. This is not what Earth looks like," he replied.

They continued exploring this unknown, weird place. Soon they saw a cottage.

"I think we can ask the people in the cottage for information about this place," suggested Buckay.

"Yeah, well what if they talk in a different language?" she asked.

"Well, there's only one way to find out."

And so, they started their journey to the cottage. Buckay was looking at the surroundings and wondering what could be like this and a very scary thought came into his mind. How would mother, father and Reyaansh know where he was, and how could he go back?

"We'd better run. I don't feel safe here and we must find the portal and get back."

"Ok," agreed Becky.

"Ok…" Buckay said.

They started running to the cottage. But on the way, Buckay dropped his phone and looked back only to see a big fierce wolf creeping behind them. He rushed back and got his phone and acted as if he had not seen the wolf.

"Becky!" Buckay called. "BECKY?!"

"Woah, stop shouting man. What happened?" asked Becky who did not know there was a wolf behind them.

"Oh, well I wanted to simply say that MY ANSWER IS BEHIND YOU!" screamed Buckay.

"Hmm, I don't think an answer should be walking around but lemme check," she said.

They took off. The wolf was catching up as it became aware they had noticed him and began to run at full speed.

"We won't be able to outrun a wolf, but we can certainly hide from it," whispered Buckay. "Look, there's a lot of tall grass right there."

"Thank God, our lives are saved," she said. They were taking wild turns and the wolf could not keep up so it just left them alone.

As soon as they realised the wolf was not chasing them, they ran to the cottage only to find out that now nothing was like pixels and they had got their normal bodies back again. But they did see a huge Chinese carnival going on near the village.

"I see no reason why we should not go," said Becky.

"So, first of all, I don't have any Chinese currency. Second of all, this is not our territory. Third of all, I don't know Chinese and fourth of all, I don't belong here nor that classroom, so we are getting out of here," said Buckay.

"Fine," she replied and they went through the portal.

Just as they entered it, Buckay returned to the park where he was taking his morning stroll and he looked around, but there was no sign of Becky. At first, he felt sad but then he went home and Reyaansh started asking where he had been for the last three hours, to which Buckay told the whole story to Reyaansh and all the family.

"And then I came back here! But sadly, Becky was not found," Buckay exclaimed as he finished narrating the story.

"Woah, that is a wonderful adventure. Hey, bro, can you show me this portal?" Reyaansh asked still unable to believe what he had just heard.

"Ok, come on let's go but I don't think it will still be there," Buckay said.

"Hmm ok," Reyaansh said, disappointed.

"Are you doubting me?" asked Buckay.

"NOPE!" replied Reyaansh, surprised.

They went to the place. Well, it surely did look like there was a portal as a lot of the park's materials had been demolished. Lucky for them, the portal was still there but perhaps lucky was not the right word. When

Reyaansh went to the portal and peeked inside, he saw a volcano! Lava was flowing towards the portal and he looked at Buckay.

"There's a volcano coming. What are we supposed to do?" Reyaansh calmly asked.

"OK, what? Why are you not scared? But anyways someone must enter the portal and only then the portal will close. I have dealt with it when I entered before but the weird thing is, why is there a volcano there now and not a classroom?"

"I do not know. All I know is that my time has come," Reyaansh said.

"No way; you are not going, I am going. Do you have powers?" Buckay asked.

"Nope, do you?" replied Reyaansh sarcastically.

"I do; now back up," Buckay said and entered the portal.

"How long will you take? I am worried about you, bro."

"At least an hour or so."

Reyaansh saluted him, unaware of what was going to happen next. He waited for an exceptionally long time which was actually just five minutes.

"Ok, I'm checking," Reyaansh thought and peeked his head inside the portal which amazingly still had not closed. To his surprise, he saw the classroom and a girl and two boys trying to open a vent. He remembered that Buckay had talked about the girl, but the boys were a snitch. So, he backed up. To his surprise, the portal was slowly shrinking! He started to panic and decided to use something to stop it shrinking and jammed it with a wooden stick.

Meanwhile, Buckay was dealing with the volcano. "AARGHH!" he groaned as his powers were too weak for the strong volcano. He decided to fly up and make a huge wall and then spray water to make the lava obsidian.

He made the wall, but the obsidian part did not work. But he was fine as it had stopped the volcano from coming out. He looked around for a portal but was unable to find it. He had been searching for more than 45 minutes and decided to give up. But just as all hope seemed to be lost, he found the portal inside the VOLCANO.

"It HAD to be in there, huh?!" Buckay shouted angrily.

He reached the top of the volcano and as he slowly and carefully went down, he noticed the portal shrinking and went a bit faster; as the portal was about to close, he went faster and faster, and he almost made it.

Reyaansh was waiting for Buckay as he saw him using his powers. He was now sure that it was something not human. He was super-excited about it. There was nothing to be scared about, right? They were brothers and had lived with each other for years. He kept getting glimpses of so many incidences where he saw Buckay using his powers and his extreme knowledge and attraction for space.

The moment Buckay came, Reyaansh asked him, "Did you develop these powers, or are you not from here, I mean Earth?"

Buckay was startled but he expected that to happen and he was ready.

"Yes, Reyaansh, I am from Thermono and my UFO crashed on Mars and from there, somehow, I reached Earth. All these years of struggle were to repair my UFO and get back to my planet. You know, right, if someone finds out I am an alien, my life will be screwed. So, the only safe thing for me is to go back to my planet. For a few months I have been sending signals to my planet UFO and recently I received a mild reply. But maybe now they know that I am here. It may be a false signal but what if it's someone from my planet? What if it's my parents or my brother?"

"Woah!" Reyaansh exclaimed. "That's a lot to take in Buckay; that's a lot."

"But the sad thing…" Buckay said.

"What is it?" Reyaansh asked, surprised.

"It is time for me to go. I will be leaving the planet in 3 weeks," Buckay said sadly.

"Are you going back to your home planet?" asked Reyaansh.

"Yes, and I might not be able to come here again."

"I am happy you are finally going to be able to see your real family and be reunited with them."

"Yes, thank you, Reyaansh but until then I have 3 weeks. Then they go back home."

"I will miss you a lot, Buckay," Reyaansh said with a tear dropping from his eye.

"I am very grateful to God that I landed in India and met you," Buckay said.

"I'm gonna miss all your stories."

"I'm gonna miss telling them to you," Buckay replied.

And so, they went back home and enjoyed dinner and had the best sleep ever.

The next day Buckay and Reyaansh went for a stroll as Reyaansh wanted to spend as much time conceivable with Buckay.

"Ok, this is so hard because every moment I just remember that you are gonna leave makes me so sad."

"Well ever since I met you, I knew myself that one day I would be leaving you, so imagine how sad I have felt," said Buckay.

"I perceive that now."

"Well, at least you're happy because I am finally meeting my parents, because I thought you would be like AAAH WHY ARE YOU LEAVING? PLEASE DON'T GO!" Buckay said and started laughing.

"Ok, well I don't think like that."

"I know, bro, chill, chill, I was joking," Buckay replied.

Then Buckay and Reyaansh went back home after a lengthy conversation during the stroll.

The next day Reyaansh woke up, brushed his teeth, ate breakfast, then went into the backyard to call a few of his friends and Buckay to come to the yard to play football. They had fun and surely Buckay and Leroy scored two goals and Reyaansh and Maxxi also two, the score was with Buckay leading by 4-3 and then, of course, Maxxi on Reyaansh's team had to score a last-minute goal and tie them.

The same day, Buckay went out for a walk, searching for Reyaansh as he had not returned yet. The wind was coming in again at super speed.

"OK, what? No way. I had somehow closed it. No way, it's BACK!" thought Buckay. And his greatest fear came true! His greatest fear was actually a tarantula, but this was way worse. The portal was OPEN!

"This is bad news," he thought. "Let me check in there really quick." He checked inside and guess what he saw? He saw his old school TCIS friends in danger and Reyaansh was up there.

"Holy cow!" Buckay said. "Yep, that explains where he was."

Reyaansh up there was holding something. Buckay climbed up the ladder and saw what the real problem was.

"WOAH! You startled me, man!" Reyaansh said. "And what are you doing up here? But I am happy that you are."

"I don't think this is the time to be asking questions," Buckay said.

The real problem was there was this HUGE- I do not mean excessively big, I mean GIGA-sized BUG!

"Is that a caterpillar?" Buckay asked.

"This is not the time to ask QUESTIONS!" Reyaansh said as the bug almost caught him.

"Hey, wait is that a sign he is holding?" Buckay asked.

"Yeah, it seems so…" Sean said. "Wait BUCKAY?! What are you doing here?"

"GOSH dang it's bro," Reyaansh said.

"It's not the TIME to ask QUESTIONS!" Reyaansh and Buckay said together.

"Oh, wait, I just noticed we are in our young age bodies," Shoban said.

"Yeah, that's weird," said Sanvi.

"Hmm, I think I know what to do," Manav said. "That thing that you are holding is called a teleportation pearl. If you get one once in your hand then you basically have infinite ones."

"Wait, so basically this thing teleports?" Reyaansh asked.

"Yes, but only you," Manav replied. "If you want everyone to get teleported together, everyone must hold hands. Where did we get this much time to talk? Why is the bug not attacking us?"

"Yeah, that is weird," Shobhan said.

Reyaansh and Buckay went to the edge to see what was happening and realised why the bug had stopped.

"Uh, guys, we have a problem," said Reyaansh.

"What is that?" asked Shreya.

"We are about to fall," replied Buckay.

"Why?" asked Gurucharan.

"THIS IS NOT THE TIME TO ASK QUESTIONS! JUST HOLD HANDS, BOYS THIS SIDE, GIRLS THIS SIDE. I'M IN THE MIDDLE cause I think I gotta stand in the middle," Reyaansh said and they quickly held hands.

The pearl went and teleported them out of there.

"Ok, I think we're safe… for now," said Reyaansh.

"Buckay, when and how did you come here?" Gurucharan asked.

"Just like you guys came here," he replied.

"By the portal?" Shreya asked.

"Yup, this is not the first time I entered the portal and don't even get me started on that."

"I saw him and that was DANGER," Reyaansh said.

Suddenly they heard a thud.

"Ok, I just must admit this," he continued, "is anyone else feeling it? So, I feel like this portal just took us back in time."

"Hmm, I agree. I do feel like that," said Shreya and everyone agreed.

THUD, BOOM, THUD, BOOM.

"Ok, we'd better get moving, 'cause those steps are coming clo-," Shobhan was interrupted by the BOOM.

"YEAH, WE GET THE IDEA, LET'S MOVE!" shouted Sean and they started running behind Buckay.

"Uh, why are we headed to the tower where the bug is?" Gurucharan asked.

"Yeah, why are we going there?" Sanjay asked who had been quiet until now.

"I am only answering this because you did not understand," replied Buckay. "First of all, the bug might not be there. Second, I came through a portal there. And third, we can climb the tower because the bug thinks we are somewhere else and if we go back to the spot we came from?"

"He will not even notice or think to check it again!" Sanjay said. "GENIUS!"

"OK," Reyaansh said, gasping for air. "If I'm going to be honest this is the first time I've heard Sanjay shout."

And everyone just agreed.

When they reached there, the portal was gone and the tower was demolished.

"Now what?" Gurucharan asked.

"We must search for more. But for now, take a break I will show you a place," said Buckay. "Reyaansh, come here," he said on the path to the resting zone. "I'm going to use my powers and make a shelter house over there."

"OK, I'll help you by telling you what to build."

Soon they arrived near a tree, and they started to sit down and chit-chat, while Buckay hurried off with Reyaansh to build a shelter home.

After at least half an hour they were done and sweating. They headed back to the place where they had left their friends.

"ALL RIGHT, SOLDIERS, follow me," ordered Reyaansh, and they followed.

"Why are we going back there?" asked Sanjay.

"'Cause we built a shelter home over there," replied Reyaansh.

"In half an hour?"

"Yeah, Buckay helped."

"Ok…"

They reached the shelter and were so happy they had some protection from any type of bug attack.

"Well at least we have some shelter," said Nainika.

Soon they started to doze off. Only Buckay and Reyaansh remained awake.

"Hey," Reyaansh called.

"Hm?" Buckay replied.

"Don't you think we should make them all hold hands just in case the bug suddenly appears?"

"Yeah, that's kind of a good idea," agreed Buckay.

"Yeah, let's do it."

They started to make everyone hold hands and Reyaansh was in the middle of them.

"I can't wait to get out of here," he said.

"Reyaansh… there are multiple chances that maybe someone or a few people might not make it," warned Buckay.

"Ay, bro, what are you talking about ma boy? That only happens in movies."

"All right," Buckay said. Then they too dozed off.

The next day it was a fresh and beautiful morning when everyone woke up and found Buckay and Reyaansh chatting.

"Hey guys," Sean whispered. "Let's listen to them?"

"Ok," everyone whispered back.

They crept a bit closer and pretended to be asleep but were listening to every word they said.

"I had a dream about us all like getting eaten up by that weird bug; that was totally weird," said Buckay.

"Hmm, I had a dreamless night," said Reyaansh.

"All right."

"Let's see if they woke up?" asked Reyaansh.

Buckay nodded sideways. "Ok, they are still asleep, pretty normal right?"

"No…" Reyaansh said.

"What do you mean?"

"Look!" Reyaansh said, pointing to their hands.

"That probably happened because they were asleep and moving," Buckay said.

"Yeah, nothing to worry about. I don't know why I was tensed."

"Hey, you know what's going on right?" Buckay asked.

"Obviously," Reyaansh said.

On the other side, those guys pretended to wake up all at once.

"I KNEW IT!" Reyaansh and Buckay said.

"What did you know?" Shreya asked.

"You were all pretending," replied Buckay.

"Oof, they found out guys," Anubhav said. "No more pranks."

"ANUBHAV!" Shobhan moaned. "We could've tricked them into believing us."

"Ha! We were gonna wake you guys up after a while anyway," Reyaansh said.

"So, what's going on right now and why were we all holding hands during our sleep?" Anubhav asked.

"Because Reyaansh and I were thinking that what if the bug came, so that's why we did it just in case," Buckay said. "If we had to run, we could not uh wake you guys up then hold hands and then go; so now you understand."

"And Buckay was watching all hands if they were not held," Reyaansh said.

"Wow, well thanks for guarding us, all," Anubhav said.

"No problem," replied Reyaansh.

"Yeah, and now we'd better move," said Buckay.

"Why?" asked Mithil.

"Oh, wait I totally forgot you were here; this is the first time you've been silent," Reyaansh said.

"OK, now can you tell us why we have to move?" Mithil asked.

"Because we have to search for the portal remember?" said Reyaansh.

They all had totally forgotten.

"Anyways me and Buckay came prepared for this situation, or should I say 'I' came prepared, Buckay?"

Buckay let out a sigh of defeat. "You, Reyaansh."

"Like?" Mithil asked.

"Like I brought a bag full of first aid kits, a laptop, walkie-talkies for 7 people and the chargers with the power bank with binoculars for more than enough."

"Woah, why did you bring all this stuff, Buckay," asked Shreya.

"Don't ask me. Reyaansh always carries this stuff and calls it backup… I never thought it would be used as backup one day, not in a million years."

"It did come in handy today so never try to tease me again, Buckay!" said Reyaansh.

"Ok, let's continue?" Shobhan said.

"This is the list of people who will receive walkie-talkies," Buckay said. "Do the honours."

"Shreya, Manav, Shubhi, Me, Buckay, and the last two do Rock, Paper, Scissors," said Reyaansh.

"Why did you pick a set of people in the first place?" asked Shobhan.

"Because when we were in 6th grade, Shreya and Manav had a phone, and they probably know how to use it," replied Reyaansh.

"Then why Shubhi?" Sean asked.

"Yeah, I don't know; there are 3 spots open and only 3 of any of you will get the phone. Are you fine with that, Shubhi?" Buckay asked.

"I'm fine with that. I might have lost the thing," Shubhi said.

Soon the Rock, Paper, Scissors were done, and Shobhan, Sanvi and Manav ended up as the winners.

Reyaansh and Buckay inserted the five-mile range covering cards into the walkie-talkies, started to try calling each other and succeeded.

"Remember we have to save the battery because we never know when it will be needed," warned Reyaansh.

Everyone understood and nodded. They started to move and split up into groups of three; each member had a phone. The groups were: Reyaansh, Buckay and Shreya. (Walkie Talkie group); Sean, Mithil and Gurucharan. (SMG group) (S= Sean M= Mithil G= Gurucharan); Sanvi, Nainika, and Sanjay. (The explorers); Harshita, Shubhi, and Shobhan. (The Brains); Anubhav, Manav and Preksha. (AMP group) (A= Anubhav M= Manav and P= Preksha).

"Wait, guys, where is Haansika?" Preksha asked.

"She did not appear here," replied Reyaansh.

"Oh, ok," said Preksha. "Wait, why did she not appear?"

"She probably did not enter the portal," Reyaansh said.

"Yeah, and also, we have already called each other on the walkie-talkies and named the channel numbers," said Buckay.

"So, guys, The Brains will go North, The Explorers, South, and we will go East. The SMG will go West, and the AMP will go Northwest," Shreya said.

"All right," agreed Buckay and Reyaansh.

"AND, wait up," said Reyaansh. "Take this; I'll give you all 3 each; use them properly only if the bug attacks. Hope the bug spray works on the bug and take these."

And so, Reyaansh gave each group a bag with three bug sprays, and three binoculars and the others just kept their walkie-talkies in their hands.

"Ok, thanks, see you at 7 back at our shelter," Anubhav said.

Meanwhile, with the Walkie Talkie group:

"Ok, this is going to be like an adventure but it's real life," announced Reyaansh.

"Yeah," replied Shreya.

"Honestly, we should collect some food so when we go back, we will have some fruit to give to our friends," suggested Buckay.

"Yeah, good idea!" said Reyaansh.

"Honestly, I never thought we would all meet like this again," said Shreya.

"Neither did I," replied Reyaansh.

"Yeah, we had a bet going," said Buckay.

"Like what?" Shreya asked.

"Like if we met again, like all together, Reyaansh would climb Mount Everest and if we didn't, I'd climb it," replied Buckay.

"Well, Reyaansh lost then," Shreya said laughing.

"Well neither and both of us lost, as Haansika is not here but everyone else is here; technically, I won but still…" Reyaansh said.

"Oh yeah," Shreya said.

Meanwhile, with the SMG group, "God, bro, why can't you just be quiet?!" Sean shouted.

"I don't know," Gurucharan replied.

"If you don't know, I'll decide it for you. Now just be quiet; only talk when you're told to or if you spot a portal," Mithil said.

"Fine," Gurucharan grumbled.

And then with The Brains:

"Well at least I understand why we are called The Brains," Shobhan tried to bring up the conversation awkwardly.

"Me too," agreed Shubhi.

"So, why are we called The Brains?" asked Harshita.

"Because we all are smart," replied Shubhi.

"Yeah… wait, wait, WAIT! GIVE ME MY BINOCULARS!" Shobhan shouted.

Shubhi gave him the binoculars and Shobhan checked through them and saw a clear portal; it was near the bug's egg, but the bug was not there.

Back with The Walkie Talkie group:

"WAIT, THERE!" Reyaansh said pointing towards a mountain. "IT'S THERE, THE PORTAL!"

"YAY, WE ARE SAVED!" Shreya shouted happily.

And as for The Explorers' group:

"OH MY GOD, THERE! THERE, OUR LIVES ARE SAVED. GET THE FRICKIN PHONE OUT!" Nainika shouted.

"WOOOO!" screamed Gurucharan.

And finally, with The AMP group:

"Wait, guys, look there," said Anubhav, "life saved."

"Oh my God, let's go there now and escape!" said Preksha.

"No," Anubhav said, smouldering.

"What do you mean?" asked Preksha.

"We must go back to Reyaansh and Buckay and tell them about the portal, or we can simply call him?" suggested Anubhav.

"Just call them and let's hurry out of here!" Preksha said.

Soon the groups called and they had all found a portal, but one of their captains, Buckay, had different plans and said, "Guys go to your portals and check inside; if we find one that takes us to Earth, we shall use that one!"

"Good idea!" said Manav.

After a few hours of work, Shreya, Buckay and Reyaansh made it up the mountain and went towards their portal.

"If we did all this for nothing, I am going to be mad, really mad," said Buckay.

"These portals contain one thing always, so if you remember, we can maybe get the kids' room," Reyaansh said.

"Yeah," agreed Buckay.

"Kids' room?" Shreya asked.

"We'll tell you about it later," said Reyaansh.

When they checked their portal, they saw three kids - two boys and one girl.

"YESSS!" shouted Reyaansh.

"Life saved," said Buckay.

"Ok, I can't wait to know about this kids' room," Shreya said.

Meanwhile, "Woah, I see a lot of cartoon characters! Woah, he's aiming his bow at me! Yes… let us get out of here," urged Manav.

Also, meanwhile,

"Inside, I see a beach full of crocodiles; no way this one," said Nainika.

Soon they all met up back at their shelter area. The walkie-talkie group came in last.

"Guys, tell us about your portals?" Shreya said.

"Ours and another 3 groups' portals cannot be entered," said Anubhav, sadly.

"Well, we can enter ours!" Reyaansh said.

"WAIT, REALLY?" asked Anubhav and everyone stood up.

"Yup," Shreya said.

"So, what's in the portal?" Sanvi asked.

"Well, there are 2 boys and 1 girl, but I have been there before, so I know how to complete that maze, but you guys need to get ready because at any moment we are gonna have to run from a speeding wolf into long grass and out," warned Buckay.

Everyone started preparing for the run. Then finally the time came.

"TIME TO ESCAPE FROM THIS PLACE!" Mithil said.

"Woo, we're getting out of here!" said Sanjay.

"Ok, is everyone ready?" asked Reyaansh.

"We have to climb a mountain," said Buckay.

"Ok, but at the top of the mountain can we take a break?" Gurucharan asked.

"I do not think we can take a risk like that," Reyaansh said. "There are chances that the portal will disappear."

"Ok," Gurucharan sighed.

They started their mountain climbing at once. It took them a long time to reach the top.

"If we climbed up here for nothing, I'm going to be really mad," warned Buckay.

"Thanks for saying that," Reyaansh said.

"What does that mean?" asked Buckay.

"Last time you said that, uh, the portal was still there; so now you're saying it so the portal will still be there?" asked Reyaansh.

"Yeah," replied Shreya.

"All right, I have a few questions right now," announced Anubhav.

"What are they?" asked Buckay.

"So how did you climb up this mountain and come down at such speed that you reached our shelter so fast?" Anubhav asked.

"Sorry, what? We came the last!" Reyaansh told Anubhav.

"But still that was kinda fast, Reyaansh."

"Well, we found a slide-type part near the mountain, so we just went sliding our way back," Reyaansh said.

"Yup, it was pretty fun," smiled Shreya.

"And last question, how did Reyaansh spot the portal without binoculars?" asked Anubhav.

"Well, it's pretty easy to spot a blue octagon with an outline of blue flames," Reyaansh said. "And I did actually check with the binoculars at the end just to confirm and, weirdly, we all found our portals at the same time; but anyways I forgot to mention I checked through the binoculars man, Anubhav you keep a lot of detail."

Anubhav nodded in agreement, and they continued to climb the mountain.

At one point, Shubhi almost fell but Sanvi and Preksha grabbed her back up and it was not easy. Finally, they had reached the top of the mountain. Sure, enough the portal was still there.

"Ok, so guys, we must all enter the portal 2+2 people at a time and quickly because the portal closes fast," said Buckay.

"Ok," said Gurucharan.

Reyaansh and Buckay were the first to go. And everyone else just simply followed, as fast as possible.

"All right, is everyone here?" Shobhan asked.

"Yes, I think so," replied Manav. "Yeah, no chance, let's count each other?"

Manav counted everyone and they all were there.

"Ok, we're safe now but we have to enter that vent. Wait before you do that; you guys wait here," insisted Buckay.

Soon the frowns on the kids' faces turned to smiles and they went over and spoke to Buckay.

"Hi, my name is Mark and that's John, and this is Becky."

"Can you help us?" asked John.

"Uh, sure."

"Thank you so much," said Becky.

Buckay opened the vent and the three kids entered but at the wrong time and they were caught by the teacher. It did not take a second for Mark and John to blame it all on Buckay for opening the vent.

"Kid, I'm really disappointed in you," said the teacher. "What's your name?"

"My name is Buckay, Ma'am, and I will not do that again as I did not know that was not to be done."

"OK, fine, but it's not to be repeated," she replied.

After the class was over, Buckay glanced at Mark and John and they immediately turned their heads away. Soon Becky came to him and apologised for her friends' behaviour.

"You don't need to apologise; let's get going from the vent now," Buckay said.

"You remember me?!" Becky asked, surprised.

"Of course."

Then Buckay and Becky opened the vent, and all the other guys came through. They had to move fast because the portal was closing again.

"All right, guys, we made it," said Buckay. "Now all we have to do is just run, at full speed!"

"Ok, just follow Buckay," shouted Shobhan.

They followed just as the wolf appeared and nearly caught up with them. Soon they reached the portal and escaped from that place but before leaving, Buckay took a quick glance outside and saw a carnival.

"Wow, I remember that," he said.

"Me too," said Becky.

"Yeah, see you later Becky!" smiled Buckay.

And they all escaped and arrived at the park where the portal was and they returned to their adult form.

"Well, at least we're still together," said Reyaansh.

"Yeah," agreed Sean.

They set off and headed to Buckay and Reyaansh's home.

"Wow, nice house, guys," said Gurucharan.

"You can all have one room shared between two," announced Buckay.

"Wait, really?" Mithil asked.

"Yes, and the second biggest guest room is for Sanjay."

"What about the first biggest one?" Shreya asked.

"That is occupied by all our stuff for inventions," replied Reyaansh.

"Oh, nice," Shreya said.

"You guys invent stuff?" asked Nainika.

"Yeah, we work for NASA," replied Reyaansh.

"Ok, what?" Sanvi asked, surprised.

"No joke," Buckay said.

Soon they all went to their rooms and called their own parents. They were going to be leaving in a week.

"Well, good night, guys," said Reyaansh.

They all said good night to each other and went to sleep.

The next day, after everyone had woken up, Reyaansh and Buckay's parents returned from their holiday trip.

"Oh, hey Reyaansh and Buckay, you invited your school friends for a while?" asked mother.

"Uh, yeah," said Reyaansh.

"Do you think they'd ever believe us?" Buckay whispered.

"The chance of them believing is low but there is a chance," Reyaansh whispered back.

"Wow, guys, your rooms are pretty good; you even have TVs in them," said Shobhan.

"Yeah, and also since Reyaansh has basically won that bet, we have some change of plans," announced Buckay.

"Like?" asked Shreya.

"Like we are giving you guys 100 pounds each," replied Reyaansh.

"Holy chaloopa!" said Nainika.

"At least we were spending our final days with our school friends," Reyaansh told Buckay.

"Yeah, I'm really happy this happened, Reyaansh."

It was a wonderful day so all of them went out for a walk to McDonalds.

"Where are we going?" Nainika asked.

"How do I know?" replied Mithil.

"Well, I know," Reyaansh said. "We're going to… MCDONALDS!"

"I've never seen anyone be that happy to go to McDonalds," Anubhav said.

"Well after this, can we go to Reyaansh and Buckay's room and watch a movie?" Shreya asked.

"Sure," said Reyaansh.

"Ok, hold up," said Buckay. "It's not 'My and Reyaansh's room'; we do not share a room we have separate."

They went to McDonalds, ate their food and went home for a movie night in Reyaansh's room before going to sleep.

They had fun for a week but then it was down to the serious business.

"Ok, soldiers," Reyaansh said.

"It's always 'soldiers' with him, isn't it?" said Shreya.

"Yes, and now Buckay and I have decided to do something for you all, sorry, us all," Reyaansh continued.

"What is it?" asked Gurucharan.

"C'est une surprise," Reyaansh said. (It is a surprise).

"I understand," Nainika said.

"We learnt French in grade 6; even I understand!" said Manav and Shreya.

"COMPRIS SOLDAT," Shreya said. (UNDERSTOOD, SOLDIER).

"Oui," said Nainika. (Yes).

"EEEENOUGHHHHHHHH FRENCH, dudes!" yelled Gurucharan.

"I agree with Gurucharan," Reyaansh said. "But we learnt French in grade 6; you've got a good memory, Manav."

"Yes," agreed Manav.

"So, people, the surprise is…" Buckay started.

"WE ARE GOING ON A HIKE!" Reyaansh exclaimed.

"Wait, actually?" Shobhan asked.

"Yeah, that's the only thing we could come up with to do for a few days, or else we're gonna be at home watching TV all day," explained Buckay.

"Ok," said Sean.

So off they went to the shop to buy some gear for camping and then bought some supplies.

"Ok, we are here so we are buying hiking sticks, jackets with safety features, a tent, a few torches and a few bug sprays," explained Reyaansh.

After a while, they were completely stacked with all the necessary items.

"Ok, so we are going tomorrow as we are all already tired because of the shopping," said Buckay.

Everyone just nodded as they were all too tired to speak and after dinner, they went to sleep.

It was time for the hike. They woke up early in the morning and got ready immediately, as this was the final week of Buckay's stay. He had sadly shortened the time by a week. Buckay and Reyaansh had invited Leroy for the hike too. As soon as he arrived, they introduced him to everyone.

"Are we all ready?" asked Reyaansh.

They set off; Reyaansh's father and mother joined them because someone would have to drive the Tesla and the Range Rover back. They had to take the Range Rover as the 2 Teslas would not fit them all in. After a long drive, they reached their destination.

"Alright, we're here!" Reyaansh shouted and it simply echoed back.

"WOOOOO!" Gurucharan screamed and again the echoes answered back.

"Well at least Gurucharan's removed all of his talking power from inside," said Nainika.

"True," Anubhav said and they started laughing.

After saying all their "goodbyes" and "be carefuls" from their mother and father, they finally started their hike. Their luck was impressive and they spotted deer almost immediately.

"Hey, look over there," Reyaansh whispered to the gang. It was a panther.

"Oh noooo!" Gurucharan whispered to them as the panther was just about to pounce on a barking deer who had not noticed it. At the last moment, Buckay threw a stone which startled both the deer and the panther. The deer began running with the panther chasing it, so they continued their hike.

"Woah look a pipe of water and there is a truck!" Gurucharan said.

"That's no pipe, Guru," said Leroy, "that's a snake."

"Oh, heck no, I'm out of here," said Gurucharan running up the hill as fast as he could and going from the side of the truck.

"I'll move the snake away from the path," said Anubhav as he gave a killer, smouldering look.

"Stop with that stupid face and don't become a hero," said Reyaansh.

"OK, OK, chill," replied Anubhav.

They continued their hike and came across a shelter house. It was not yet dark, so they continued.

"Ahh, I'm starting to get tired," groaned Leroy.

Everyone agreed. Finally, they reached a place where they did not have to climb anymore, with a straight and clear path. It was starting to get dark, so they set their tents and went inside to sleep. Not what you would imagine, no lighting a fire, roasting marshmallows and having a conversation; they were just too tired. Soon the night passed and it was time for them to move on. So, they packed up their tents and continued.

While crossing the river, Nainika looked back and saw a water snake.

"Oh my God guys, look there!" Nainika pointed to the snake.

"YEAH, WE BETTER MOVE FAST!" Leroy shouted.

"Why are you shouting?" asked Buckay.

"It's got speed, Buckay!" he replied.

"Eh, not sure about that."

"Wanna be sure?"

"No thanks, Leroy, I'm good," said Buckay, laughing.

They continued on their path and reached an old, abandoned junkyard.

"Hmmm, what type of place can this be?" Shreya asked.

"It's a junkyard," Reyaansh told her.

They saw a few broken cars and trucks, but this was the end of their hike. It was on top of the hike where they found this junkyard. They took pictures and enjoyed the view for a while and then started to go down. They got down easily and fast because they did not have much time left to be with Buckay.

"Hey Reyaansh…" Buckay called.

"Yeah?" Reyaansh asked without turning his head because he was hiding that tiny tear that had formed in his eyes.

"I just wanted you to know that you can tell our friends about me being an alien because I think they are kind-hearted and deserve to know and this is my last day sadly."

"Yeah, I'll let them know," Reyaansh said sadly, now the tear had fallen, and more were forming. "I will always be waiting for you Buckay."

"And I will always be hoping to see you again," said Buckay.

After they reached the bottom of the hike, they went into the cars and Reyaansh told the story of Buckay being an alien and waited for them to reach home so he could prove it to them as well.

"Here guys, here is the proof. Buckay, show it to them," Reyaansh said.

"Yeah…" said Buckay and he converted back into an alien. He looked so different but amazing. Everyone was stunned.

"What are you guys gonna do?" Reyaansh asked.

"WHAT?" Gurucharan exclaimed.

"Since we have lived with you and studied with you, we know you are a good alien; you have good intentions, we know we can trust you, Buckay, 😊 " said everyone.

"And I trust you all, too!" exclaimed Buckay.

"Hey that's what I said when I first found out about him being an alien," said Reyaansh.

"Yeah, well we still have to tell mother and father," said Buckay.

"So…" Reyaansh said.

The whole story was narrated to the family and proof given and the sad news was delivered to the entire family and friends.

"But wait, Buckay, how will you reach your parents? Son, I am worried about you," asked mother.

Father was speechless with all the mixed emotions. Nurvi Just hugged Buckay and mother and tears fell down her cheeks. Buckay felt the emotions and hugged his mum, father, and sister from Planet Earth.

"Well, Buckay told me to keep this a secret from all of you reading this and mother and father that he had been secretly fixing his UFO, as he had become friends with an expert at NASA and had built his UFO with different machines and fuel, so it was now, way faster," explained Reyaansh.

"How do you know if your parents are waiting for you?" asked Leroy, "not in a negative way."

"Well let's hope for the best, Leroy!" said Buckay.

"OK, everybody, I have something to say," Buckay announced. "I just wanted to let you guys know a few things. Reyaansh you are the true meaning of amazing, kind, friendly and of course good at keeping secrets as well. Leroy, you were always there for me, and we had a lot of fun inventing stuff. I will always remember those good old *Diwali*, *Holi*, Christmas, Halloweens, and of course birthdays.

"Mother and father, you were the best. If not for you I would have never been able to be what I am today. You guys, my good friends from India, I will never forget you and the good times we had. Last but not least, Nurvi. You were there when I was sad, to cheer me up."

Everyone had tears in their eyes.

After a while, Buckay took Reyaansh to the side of the room and gave him the gun which opened the portals.

"Buckay, what is this?" Reyaansh asks surprised.

"This is the gadget which will help in opening up portals if you ever need them. After all, you need to send our friends back, right?"

"Thank you Buckay!"

The launch started.

"I will miss you a lot, Buckay!" screamed Reyaansh and Leroy.

"I will miss you more than you will!" Buckay shouted back.

The launch commenced and with a flash, Buckay was off to space. He landed on the moon after few days and started sending signals to Thermono, just in case, to know if his parents were back.

"Beh too kept sehp sha sho rad Thermono?" This was Buckay's signal. sent. (Did my parents reach Thermono?)

"Idesty kisa," the alien replied. (Identity please).

"Ah Buckay Lemos too kept eh Crisco Lemos oar Kianchi Lemos rad," Buckay replied. (Ah Buckay Lemos; did my parents Crisco Lemos and Kianchi Lemos reach?)

"Ahsi hir," the alien told him. "Saht dued ki da eys sid ahis lif fer 9 uers (No sir, it seems they did not come for 9 years.)

Buckay was surprised at the amount of time he had spent on Earth.

Horrific thoughts entered his mind but only one mattered: "Are they alive...?"

Signed: The robot of UFO 2039475729. (Master Buckay Crisco Lemos).

– TO BE CONTINUED –

***

The Good Aliens' UFO converts into a pendant.
And for each UFO they all have a robot.
It is an observatory robot.
It records everything that is in view of it.
That robot is the one narrating the story.

***

Acknowledgements

To my parents, Deepty and Kaustubh for their trust in me to write this book.

To my entire family who loves me immensely and appreciates me for my simple achievements, I really wish to make them greatly proud of something that I do.

And last but not least, my dear sister, Nurvi. After all, the Alien's name came out of her mouth when she was just one and a half years old. Whenever she saw anything bright and shiny, she used to say "Buckay!" I decided that I would cherish this word and if I ever invented anything, I would name it Buckay.

To Keith and Caroline for trusting my work and making my book happen.

About the Author

Introducing Reyaansh Joshi, 12 years old, who received high praise from his teacher for his exceptional imagination and ability to vividly describe a whole range of situations.

Reyaansh, a sports enthusiast, enjoys playing tennis, football and chess. Having relocated to Britain seven months ago, he was fortunate to have a three-month break before starting school. He spent this time productively and managed to finish writing this novel.

The author's journey in India was filled with thrilling tales of adventures with his companions. Sharing these enchanting stories with his mother led her to suggest he try writing a novel.

It was then that he discovered his natural talent for writing, confirming his abilities and igniting his passion to pursue it further.

Look out for Part 2 of *An Alien's Biography* and other adventures.

You can reach Reyaansh Joshi on –

president.blue2.0@gmail.com

Instagram – Author Reyaansh Joshi

*Available worldwide from Amazon
and all good bookstores*

———————

www.mtp.agency

www.facebook.com/mtp.agency

@mtp_agency

www.ingramcontent.com/pod-product-compliance
Lightning Source LLC
LaVergne TN
LVHW091934070526
838200LV00068B/988